MAPLEDORUM TRINKET,

SUPPOSEDLY,

DREAMS

IN

RAINBOWS.

A VERY SHORT STORY

BY

LOUIS L. LASSER IV

Daydreaming at Midnight llc

Publishers

New York

FOREWARD,

BACKWARD, UP, AND DOWN

MAPLEDORUM TRINKET,
SUPPOSEDLY,
DREAMS IN RAINBOWS,
is a larger-than-life story. This is not as grandiose an introduction as it appears because Mapledorum was *"the smallest man in america."* For him, everything was larger than life. (Note: The officials who had the authority to bestow such a moniker thought it quite a bit of fun to exclude all capital letters from his title.) Nevertheless, Mapledorum wore the golden thimble gallantly until the first of January, 1932. For reasons to be explained in this account, his reign was—as it were—cut short. He welcomed his sudden estrangement from the circus of royalty. This is because Mapledorum was in love… with desire. The only crowns he was interested in wearing belonged on his teeth.

"Ultimately, it is the desire,
not the desired,
that we love."

FRIEDRICH WILHELM NIETZSCHE

DEDICATION

FOR
ELIZABETH ACAMPORA

Thank you for inspiring me to reach greater heights, even
when I'm leaning down to pick up my linen napkin from the
floor. You make time travel more fun, whether forward in
fifty-nine second increments, or in imagined lives independent
of the lunar revolutions. May both your dreams and wishes be
silly and true.

begins with an untangled infinity sign,
asserts her identity under the crescent moon dot in the sky,
and ends with a zap of beauty and lightning.

Mapledorum Trinket, Supposedly, Dreams in Rainbows.

A Very Short Story

by
Louis L. Lasser IV

ABCD E FGHIJK L MN O PQRSTU V WXYZ

ZYXW V UTSRQP O NM L KJIHGF E DCBA

CHAPTERS

INDIGO

NEW YEAR'S DAY 1900
ALL HALLOWS' EVE 1925

LOLLIPOP

NEW YEAR'S EVE 1925

PETITE LARCENY

BLACK THURSDAY 1929

MYSTISSIPPI

CHRISTMAS EVE MORNING 1929

THE LAP MAGICIAN

CHRISTMAS EVE EVENING 1929
CHRISTMAS DAY NIGHT 1929

OMEGABET

BOXXXING DAY 1931
NEW YEAR'S DAY 1932
JANUARY THE SECOND SECOND 1932

AFTERWARD,

BEFOREWARD, DOWN, AND WAY, WAY, UP

.INDIGO.

"No one ever made a difference by being like everyone else."

P.T. BARNUM

I

NEW YEAR'S DAY
1900

WALNUT, INDIANA

Mapledorum Trinket was born at sunset under the shell of a circus tent, specifically under the indigo triangle of the rainbow big top. The other colors of the spectrum were present both under the canopy and in the watercolor sky above it. Since the indigo triangle had a small tear in the fabric, Mapledorum realized the possibility that there may be a loose seam in the heavens as well. Even as a newborn, he had perspective. He quickly learned just how small one's life can feel in the shadow of the infinite. And this was only the tenth of it.

His mother was a sideshow performer. Standing at six inches tall, six-and-a-half inches with heels, her stage name was "The Diminutive Damsel in Distress." Her act involved being tied to the tracks of a model train set. For the first twenty-five years of his life, she and Mapledorum traveled the thunderous railways across the continental United States in paths of slow lightning bolts.

By this time, Mapledorum had grown to the identical stature as his mother, although, he never wore heels. But he did have an act of his own. It was modeled after the final scene of the silent film, "Safety Last!" In the scene, the headlining actor, Harold Lloyd, scales a tall building, which culminates in a gymnastic and hysteric effort to resist gravity's desire. He grasps on to the hands of a large clock, possibly to save himself, or possibly, to turn back to the time before he made this attempt. In Mapledorum's act, his little fingers latch on to the hands of a pocket watch.

ALL HALLOWS' EVE
1925

NOBLE, OKLAHOMA

On the eve of November, the Diminutive Damsel met her final distress, dying of an acute heart attack while bound to the tracks. Mapledorum watched her last scene in despair as she stopped struggling to loosen the ties that bound her to the planet. He imagined her soul ascending to heights unseen, slipping through an indigo seam in the circus tent that surrounds our reality, and veils us from the ideas of new colors and enlightened ways of seeing.

Mapledorum asked one of the lion tamers to dig him a grave. He asked the snake charmer for one of her jewelry boxes. She brought him a long box with a necklace inside. The string had broken years ago and she hadn't had the time to repair it. So, he buried his mother, still in her costume and tied in slip knots, on a bed of unstrung pink beads rounded by centuries of tidal changes on the banks of the Nile River.

When the circus boarded their train, heading to another town dusted by desperation, he stayed behind, ready to find a tear in his own linen sky, perhaps lined with silver. Or at least, silverware. Mapledorum was already hungry. The locomotive rumbled west, and he set his sights to the east. In the wake of the wind swirling from the end of the caboose, one of the show's posters spun in a tempest before landing on the ground in front of him.

P.T. BARNUM'S

GREATEST SHOW ON EARTH

PRESENTING

THE PHANTASMIC PHENOMENA OF THE PHONETICALLY FANTASTIC AND THE BAFFLING BIOLOGY OF THE BIZARRE!

FEATURING

"THE DIMINUTIVE DAMSEL IN DISTRESS"
"PINEAPPLE-HEAD BOY"
"CAVITY PATTY"
"CLUTTERFINGERS"
"TOPSY-CURVY"
"THE SMALLEST MAN IN AMERICA"
"DOE-RE-MI, THE THREE-HEADED SONGSTRESS"
"FLICKER-LICKING LILITH, THE FIRE BREATHER"
"SABRE SADIE, THE SWORD SWALLOWER"
"CLEOSNATCHRA, THE SNAKE CHARMER"
AND
BLIND PALM READINGS
WITH THE
MAJESTIC AND MYSTIC
MS. MISSY MISSISSIPPI

YOUR CURIOSITY COMMENCES
THURSDAY, SEPTEMBER 22

Mapledorum left a trail of his sandy footprints over it, each the size of the poster's smallest font, on his way to the shimmering beacon of opportunity, New York City. He'd had enough of the sideshow business, anyway. He had aspirations of his own. He wanted to be an oral surgeon.

LOLLIPOP

"I haven't been out of work
since the day I took my pants off."

SALLY RAND

NEW YEAR'S EVE
1925

LOWER EAST SIDE, MANHATTAN

Once Mapledorum was on his own and without the protection of those who knew him best—meaning the ones who knew to watch where they stepped—he felt his true size for the first time. He was kicked, booted, high-heeled, and Mary-Janed around for months. The bruisings wore off, but the mental hematoma was beginning to shade his optimism. Perhaps indigo was not his color after all.

Finding a proper dental education proved to be difficult. The universities didn't know how to deal with him. When he would climb up the wall to the registrar's window, he'd be met with gasps before being ushered out. On his last effort, at least the registrar spoke to him. She stuttered nervously, "I don't think it's polite to just walk in here like that! This is a university, for goodness sake!" Then she skittered off and crouched behind a filing cabinet, with the hope that he would just leave.

But Mapledorum was going to make sure he was heard this time. He crawled under the separation glass, and politely, yet sternly, asserted his aspirations to the registrar. He told of his days in the circus and of his mother's passing.

The registrar's head emerged, next to the drawer labeled P-Q. But Mapledorum noticed that she'd been covering her ears. So he yelled at the top of his pomegranate seed-sized lungs, "I want to be an oral surgeon! I want to contribute to science and the medical profession! And I want to learn about my rare condition! I want to uplift humanity in the same way I lift up myself!" Raising his small index finger, he punctuated his comments with frustration, "I've had it up to here with you people!"

The registrar unfortunately, yet understandably, started laughing herself into a wheezing frenzy.

"Oh, so funny that was for you! You think I haven't already heard it all?!" Mapledorum scaled the coatrack next to her desk in a fit of rage. He gripped his way to the top, battling through silk scarves and raincoats, using buttonholes and lapels for leverage. When he reached the summit, he looked down at the registrar with triumph and defiance. He watched her rise to the level of the A-B drawer, then pull herself up using the top of the filing cabinet. Now, the two climbers were nearly at the same eye level. Mapledorum didn't really know what to expect, but he was surprised to see that she was wearing the same look as one of the circus audience members. She was in awe.

When she asked Mapledorum how he would like to make his deposit payment, he told her it would take about a year to lug it all in. She said it had to be paid that day by 5:00 PM, as it was the last day of registration.

Mapledorum hung his head low, slid down the sleeve of a blue parka, and landed on her desk. He kicked a pencil out of frustration and broke his big toe. Even with the swelling, it was still very little. The registrar wished him well and hoped she'd see him return next semester.

Mapledorum hadn't considered the feats of logistical prowess he would've had to plan for. To carry rolled-up bills and silver dollars from his temporary quarters in Washington Square Park, especially after a hard day's work, would've proven to be a strongman's task. But after witnessing the efforts of his fellow circus performers, he knew how to use his legs and save his back. Of course, it didn't matter at this point. He still had to land a job.

So Mapledorum carried on without having to bear the weight of modernistic expenses. He decided to appeal directly to practicing dentists. He boasted about his potential to be a very detailed hygienist, to closely assess abscesses, and his ability to reach into the mouth of a patient, and extract a root firsthand, and if it was stubborn, a second hand. He had in the past, with much success, done this for his fellow freaks of nature while they traveled from one town to the next. Alas, no one was willing to take him on as an apprentice. They didn't want their practice to become part of a sideshow either.

Mapledorum pursued other jobs and landed a few, inching closer to his goal of financial stability, or at least, financial predictability. He worked as a fruit fly exterminator, a piano tuner, and a dollhouse interior decorator. He also had a short stint, pardon the expression, as a mechanic. But one day, when he climbed into the engine to change a spark plug, someone turned the keys and stepped on the gas. It was the scariest and oiliest moment of his life.

Then he dreamed of becoming the owner of his own company, albeit a company of one. It would specialize in dusting and sanitizing all the hard-to-reach areas. He marketed his services in inventive ways. He made business cards by cutting stamps in half and glueing his information to the front. Then he'd place them under appliances in restaurant kitchens, on the inside of violins at concert halls, or under the typewriter keys in a newspaper office.

You Missed a Spot!
~
Mapledorum Trinket
Proprietor

The obvious trouble was that no one could find the energetic entrepreneur when they wanted to hire him. Mapledorum's business was swept clean, and under the rug. So he dropped his little mop, and picked up the telephone with the help of a friend, naturally. He answered a newsprint ad in a Manhattan publication and successfully landed a position as a private eye. He proved to be an asset, with his stakeout locations winding up in places never thought to be possible from the vantage of the naked eye. From the first time he heard his boss use it, Mapledorum enjoyed the term, *the naked eye*. He'd mutter to himself on his commute, pretending to be a character on a radio show, "Sir, you've been caught by Mr. Trinket, the private eye with a keen naked eye." Or, "When Mapledorum is in town, you better not be caught with your pants down. He will privately eye your naked lie." Or, "Mr. Trinket, the naked private eye with plenty of places to hide."

Despite the fact that his eyelids only had to blink over the surface area of a peppercorn, his vision was superior to those tall enough to ride rollercoasters. This came without shock, as they had been since birth. But he lacked the physical power to press the shutter on the camera without audible grunts. Subsequently, he was discovered by one of his targets, and then he was let go by his boss. At the same time, his comfortable underground lodging in Washington Square Park was being compromised by an influx of new construction.

Then, when Mapledorum was again pondering the phrase, *the naked eye*, had a moment akin to the one Adam and Eve had in the Garden of Eden. He looked at himself in the reflection of a discarded milk bottle and saw that he was indeed, unclothed. Except for a few sprinkles of body hair, he was bare. His berries were not buried and his twig lacked a leaf to act as a sheath. He was rudely nude. Looking back, he realized that not wearing clothes may have been the chief hinderance regarding his efforts to be educated and employed. The circus had been far more accepting of the birthday suit dress code. And on second thought, maybe that explained some of the success of his circus act, adding to the fulfilled curiosity of the attendees.

So, on his walk toward a home that would soon no longer exist, he set out to find new lodgings. And some pants.

But first, he needed a weapon. And in that moment, something landed in front of him like a miracle wrapped in pink paper. It was a lollipop.

PETITE LARCENY

"Comfort is the enemy of progress."

P.T. BARNUM

BLACK THURSDAY 1929

WASHINGTON SQUARE PARK, MANHATTAN

The lollipop was in between two school children. They had been arguing over who was going to enjoy the sugared dream of sticky salivation. They had a quick game of tug of war and the lollipop landed on the battlefield. While they continued their spat over whose spit would be artificially pinkened, Mapledorum took cover in a drain that clung to a skyscraper like a great white beanstalk. He covered his own magic beans, keenly aware of his nakedness now, and because they were children. There'd been a sun shower not too long ago and some of the water had yet to find its way to the ground from the rooftop.

He saw the two sets of legs hop backward and forward, the result of their shoving each other. When there was an opportunity, Mapledorum, acting like the vermin he'd soon live amongst, sprinted out from the drain, grabbed the candy stick, and retreated to the damp safety of a trickling urban waterfall. The schoolchildren were shocked to see that they were now fighting over nothing. They walked away, deprived of their afternoon jolt of joy. Mapledorum was armed and ready for the fight before him.

Beginning a life of petit larceny—or in his case, petite larceny—was never his plan. But it seemed that life's circumstances put him in this tight spot, which he hoped would eventually land him in the tight pockets and unzipped pocketbooks of the members of high society.

After the sun disappeared between the canyons of capitalism — on the same day the stock market supernova exploded, bringing the darkness of night to the break of pay — Mapledorum scaled the wall of an apartment building, looking for points of entry. Other unfortunate souls were taking the opposite route, falling in the same direction of the charts, and bursting bubbles they became.

Mapledorum struck gold when he happened upon a couple who were getting ready to spend a night out on the town. The only thing they ever invested in was each other. He heard them tell their daughter that she'd be staying with her neighboring friend across the hall. Once their living room lights dimmed, Mapledorum's face lit up.

He found his way to their bathroom and scaled the side of their clawfoot bathtub. There was still a puddle of soapy water at the bottom. He bathed, splashed around, and pretended to be Babe Ruth sliding into home. He felt like a new man. Getting out of the tub wasn't easy. The suds on his body and the sleek porcelain tub were a slippery duo. Eventually, Mapledorum dried himself off and got to work.

He found some loose change, but he told himself he would only resort to stealing coins if he were desperate. Climbing down the side of a building while holding the equivalent of a set of car tires would be less than ideal. Paper money was really the only way to go. Mapledorum looked in some obvious places, but came up empty. Then, under the couple's bed, he found a small metal box. He reached into the keyhole and manipulated the gears with surgical acumen. He pried it open and kept it ajar with his lollipop stick. Mapledorum thought he found God, but really, he found eighty-two dollars. On Black Friday, even God knew better than to hide it in a safe. It was nearly a month's salary. He rolled the bills up like a carpet and tucked them under his arm.

The door to the girl's bedroom was closed, but Mapledorum, now moving with confidence, decided to squeeze himself under the door. It was uncomfortable, but he managed. The head of the lollipop was too big to take with him. He didn't think there would be anything to find there, but he was as wrong as he had ever been. The city's constellation of window lamps provided enough light for him to see that he'd stepped foot right into a dollhouse.

There were three dolls in the open-faced home. Like a mini version of the family, there was a man, a woman, and a little girl. When he looked at the woman, he blushed. Even though she was a mannequin, she was attractive, and just the right height. He took her by the hands and sang her a little tune he'd learned on the circus tour from a woman with three heads. Her stage name was Doe Re Mi. Of course, she sang it to him with the harmonies of an alto, a mezzo soprano, and a true soprano. Mapledorum spun the doll around and ended with a dip on the last note of the song. And he kissed her. It was the first one he ever gave anyone. Mapledorum wiped a few tears from his face, walked her over to the couch, and positioned her comfortably.

As for the man, things weren't going to be so sweet. Mapledorum shoved him to the ground and took off his clothes. He pulled on a pair of gray trousers and slipped into a blue work shirt. The hat didn't fit, but he felt they restricted free thinking, anyway. About to be on his way with a romantic lightness to his footsteps, he suddenly felt a blanket of danger around him. He looked around on high alert. Mapledorum thought he was being watched. He breathed a little sigh of relief when, in a dark corner of the girl's room, meaning the large room, he saw a lineup of stuffed animals, their eyes with little sparkles of refracted light. As he bid them adieu, one of them blinked. Mapledorum stiffened into an awkward pose, trying to fit in with the rest of the members of the dollhouse.

It was the family cat. It was real, fluffy, and predatory.

During his days on the tour, he'd been around lions, lionesses, tigers, and tigresses. But they were tamed by his fellow world travelers. They weren't anything like the domestic beast in front of him. The house cat pounced, and the dollhouse became a bouncy house. Mapledorum jumped into the bathroom and picked up the mini clawfoot bathtub to protect himself from the foot claws of the cat. In a panic, he threw the bathtub at the feline demon. It bought him just enough time to climb upstairs to the little girl's little bedroom. The cat hissed, and in his brand new pants, Mapledorum pissed. The cat swiped right into the little bedroom, tore through his shirt, and lacerated his skin. So much for the aspirations of being a fashion darling.

Mapledorum rolled like a log under the bed for protection, but he got caught up in the curtain that he inadvertently pulled off the wall. It bound his arms to his sides. The cat aimed its yellow eyes at him like the high beams on the front of a furry locomotive. His life flashed before him and the cat lashed after him. He closed his eyes and imagined the tear in the indigo sky at the beginning of his life—and the primal tears into the fabric of his skin. And then he thought of his mother. He internalized the struggles of "The Diminutive Damsel in Distress," both on the tracks of the model train set, and the parallel lines of their parallel life stories. He was not going to let the Trinket lineage end this way.

Mapledorum's veins caught fire and he broke free from the curtain. He picked up the bed and took a home run swing that caught the cat's paw. The cat retracted. He continued his attack, raging through the house, upending tables, and finding weapons to launch at the beast. If only he had his lollipop, he thought. He threw the ice box and nicked one of the cat's marbles. He tugged a handful of whiskers from its face. And then he hurled a grandfather clock that clocked the cat a few seconds back. Mapledorum was about to make his escape, but the cat made one last lunge. With its fangs out and a gust of cat food breath, he had no other choice but to sacrifice the little girl. Mapledorum shoved the little doll into the cat's mouth and ran for freedom. As he squeezed himself under the door, the cat got in a few more vicious swipes.

In the hallway of safety, any feelings of guilt he imagined he'd have about being a thief, were replaced by elation, and the thrill of survival. But there was one problem. The money was still inside the room on the living room floor of the dollhouse. With the cat still pawing at the door, looking for another round, Mapledorum decided to cut his losses.

He knew right then and there, that this was not the way he was going to live his life. He welled up and shed more tears, partly on account of his allergy to the feline's dander. With tattered, blood-stained, and urine-infused clothes, he dragged the head of his lollipop across the floor before slinging it over his shoulder. Mapledorum was utterly bummed. As for the lollipop, it was the most depressing experience a piece of candy has ever had.

Mapledorum chuckled in spurts over the sounds of his sobbing when he realized that a professional cat burglar he would not become. As he was leaving through the window, he heard the apartment door open and the little girl walk inside with her neighboring friend. They were there to feed the cat and retrieve her dolls for the sleepover. Mapledorum was sure she'd have some complaints about the new interior decorating in her dollhouse. It had been one of his jobs after all. And thankfully for him, the cat would still have its appetite.

This wasn't a life lesson. This was a death lesson.

Mapledorum walked the midnight streets of New York City and looked for a place to stay. Along the way he was harassed by several creatures of the night. He'd reached a nadir, so he had little issue using his weapon to knock out a mouse with one swing, stun a spricket's antennae, or joust a wayward gerbil.

Eventually, he happened upon an ignored basement near Pennsylvania Station. Mapledorum found a way in and slept in a cozy depression in the old cold floor, furthering his descent. After a month of Sundays and vantablack nights, Mapledorum was growing tired of his rodent bedfellows. He even befriended one of them who was missing an eye and a leg, still drawn to the curiosities of the planet. But after a night when he saw what the rat dragged in, which was the carcass of the cat he'd recently battled, no doubt kicked to the curb by the family after it destroyed the home within their home, he rose from the bed, and hit the road. He held the lollipop stick over his shoulder. Hanging from the end of the stick were his few belongings and two days of literal junk food tied up in the wrapper. It took him a long time to lick that lolly clean from the stick, even though he always did. He didn't like to waste anything except time.

This was about to change, however. So tired he'd become of watching his life move in the opposite direction of his past ambitions. He'd always been a climber, a showman, a small and wondrous attraction.

MYSTISSIPPI

"I swing big, with everything I've got.
I hit big or I miss big.
I like to live as big as I can."

GEORGE HERMAN "BABE" RUTH

CHRISTMAS EVE MORNING
1929

HERALD SQUARE PARK, MANHATTAN

In the present tense, Mapledorum is taking a walk toward a pretense. He sees a sign.

BLIND PALM READINGS

THE TRUTH LIES IN CONTRADICTION'S BED

THE MAJESTIC AND MYSTICAL MS. MISSY MISSISSIPPI

NONSENSE IS THE ONLY SENSE

He remembers her from the circus tour. Mapledorum also knows she isn't actually blind. She was said to have an unusual case of ocular dysmorphia. If she were to take off the seven pairs of glasses she wears at time, her vision will be nearly supreme. Ms. Mississippi believes that it's easier to see into the future, only if one cannot see what is right in front of them. Her reasoning is not incorrect, for to see what is in front of you, you can only look into the past. For example, the nanosecond that it takes for the light to reflect off the palm of your hand and reach your eyes, still counts on the universal clock. As a rule of physics, the speed of light takes time. Even in *the now*, you're really seeing your hands in the very recent past.

Since Ms. Mississippi can't see them at all, she's taken one of the possible ways of seeing out of the equation. By her logic, what she will *see* when she's reading someone, can only be the fleeting present, or the eventual future. She knows that she'll either be *in* step, or one step ahead.

Ms. Mississippi also wears seven pairs of gloves. Most people claim that she is making traditional palm reading a ruse. In this case, *most* people are correct. On the other hand —my apologies—the rest of the people claim that palm reading always has been a ruse. In this case, the rest of the people are not wrong. Nevertheless, she believes that if you actually touch something, you can't feel it. Try taking that one on as a philosophical dance partner. And if you complain to her about it, the southern belle won't hear anything of it! This is because she stuffs seven cotton balls into the pair of ears on her head. Ms. Mississippi believes that if you hear someone speak, their language will disrupt the message they are trying to send. Ms. Mississippi is a slippery character with banana peels for shoes.

Despite all of this, Mapledorum walks into her realm, a closet-sized storefront that seems to be holding up a large, crooked building. There are no candles, no ornamentation, and no wind chimes. There is simply a long table and two chairs. Ms. Mississippi sits on one side and Mapledorum climbs up onto the chair opposite the mystic, who looks poised to perform an operation on a radioactive hyena.

She says, "Show me your palms."

Mapledorum keeps them on his lap, directly over his fake pockets.

"Ahhh, yes. I see, I don't see. You're pretending to be shy, but you're the one who walked in here. Please, by all means, keep your hands on your lap."

Mapledorum stands up and places his hands on the table, palms up.

"Defiant and skeptical you are. Hmmm... You must be someone who has traveled a great distance to be here."

Mapledorum arches an eyebrow like an inchworm arches its back.

"You never thought I'm the real deal, did you?"

Mapledorum looks over his shoulder.

"Don't worry, there's no one else here. Hmmm... That's the problem, isn't it? You're not looking for your future; you're looking for your now."

Mapledorum nods his head in silence.

Ms. Mississippi senses the positive aura emitting from his mind. "You know where you want to go, but you fear you'll get there alone."

Mapledorum closes his eyes.

"You, my dear, are looking for love."

Mapledorum opens his eyes, brings his palms toward himself, and studies the lines. His fingers relax and he brings them together, forming a bowl.

"You won't find love by looking from above. You find love by holding it above everything else, including yourself."

Mapledorum, keeping his hands in a bowl shape, lifts them up in front of the warm indigo light emanating from the chandelier overhead. In between his pinky fingers is a gap, or as he sees it, a small tear in the atmosphere of his own creation.

"You see? Your future lives in the presence of your first revelation from the past."

Mapledorum lets down the sky and holds it over his heart.

"I'm going to grant you one wish. But it will only come true if you don't believe it will."

Mapledorum makes his wish in a quiet thunder clap of thought. He tries to remain incredulous, literally hoping against hope.

"But I can't do everything myself. There is something *you* must do. You'll know what it is when it is not there." Ms. Mississippi performs an incantation with balletic and parabolic gestures. While writing in the air with her well-gloved finger, she says, "Absĕdeff! Gīge! Klĕm! Nŏp! Quirce! Toove! Wicks! Wise!"

Mapledorum, upon hearing such silliness, loses all hope and faith that there is any merit to this charade.

Ms. Mississippi isn't done. She says the spell again, as one phonetically cohesive word. "Absĕdeffgīgeklĕmnŏpquircetoovewickswise!" Her finger writes in the warm atmosphere with urgency before her improvised pen points at her lips, and then at her heart.

Mapledorum, as if possessed by an unseen force, also points to his heart. He realizes it's not so much beating, but vibrating. It feels as if it's growing inside him and trying to expand his ribcage.

"If you're wondering what that was, which you are, I'll tell you. It's something you've known for as long as you can recall. It's the alphabet said as one word."

Mapledorum tries to say the first ten letters in his head and gives up quickly.

She continues, again reciting the alphabet as one word. "abcdEfghijkLmnOpqrstuVwxyz. It represents the origin of all words and the infinite possibilities thereafter. It means anything you want it to be, and it means everything you wish it wasn't. But the word's first order of responsibility, is to hold LOVE within it, and to keep it safe. Why else would it keep LOVE guarded with such a militarized structure and symmetry? It has four letters on each end to protect E and V from an outside attack, abcd to the west, zyxw to the east. Then it built a fortress of six letters between the next two, fghijk before you can get to L, utsrqp before you can get to O. And just for good measure, it stuck mn between them, like three arches of support. It even keeps LOVE out of order, as to further veil its importance."

As if a perfume bottle with a visible fragrance appears above the table, Mapledorum sees the word in the midst of the mist.

ABCD EFGHIJK LMN O PQRSTU V WXYZ

Ms. Mississippi finishes her thoughts by saying, "The language of LOVE is the presence of all the possible beautiful things you can write and say to someone you care for."

The wingspan of Mapledorum's attention is wider than all the birds in the sky.

She says sternly, "Now leave this place. Go and find beauty in rainbows!"

Mapledorum doesn't move. He's flying high in thought.

She raises her voice and it jostles Mapledorum's serenity. "I don't mean next week… I mean now! Go and find beauty in rainbows!" She senses he's put his hands back down on the table, leaving his heart vulnerable, which is the safest place for it. She continues, "Now listen… I'm going to take off my glasses, one pair at a time. And if I see you, I will know you aren't really here in this profound moment. If I don't see you, I will know you are exactly where you're supposed to be."

And with that, Mapledorum dashed to Pennsylvania Station, and the train dashed to the east.

Definition

abcdef·ghij·klm·nop·qrs·tuv·wx·yz /ˈabsĕdeffˈgīgeˈklĕmˈnŏpˈquirceˈto oveˈwicksˈwise/

▸ **n.** The genesis and protector of love.

THE LAP MAGICIAN

"You are extraordinary within your limits, but your limits are
extraordinary!"

GERTRUDE STEIN

CHRISTMAS EVE EVENING 1929

LONG ISLAND, NEW YORK

On the train, Mapledorum is watching the patches of oaks, elms, and firs fly by like the pages of a flip book. The trees look happy. And then he watches the maples blur by—the reflection of himself in the window included—and they look like they feel… sappy. He watches suburbia rise and fall in between stations. He reads the signs of businesses pitching vacations. He's looking for a rainbow, but it's one of those dry days where the clouds are hiding from sun rays. He's looking for something beautiful. He's looking for what's beyond the newest tear in fabric-sphere.

Mapledorum's improvised seat on the window sill is uncomfortable. So he prays, crosses his legs, and hopes to lie. But he's afraid he'll slip off and land on the seat below. A bed of feathers it is not. He uncrosses his legs and curses their existence. He resigns to recline, using his neck as his pillow. Mapledorum watches the Long Island landscape in shorter waves. While he starts to drift off, he thinks that maybe this is all wrong.

Mapledorum's eyes blink open like a nervous oyster, shy about revealing the pearl within. He sees something that captures his attention. There's a string of businesses similar to the ones he'd see on a city avenue, but they're missing the stories of apartments above them. The signs are in a row, but they're not in alignment. They're more like uneven bricks with different typefaces.

PSYCHIC READINGS   *The Beauty Mark*   SUPPOSEDLY. IN RAINBOWS.   *PHOTOGRAPHIC MEMORIES*

And right there in the middle, Mapledorum discovers the three words that he is meant to find: *Beauty in Rainbows*. He whispers them in sounds never before seen.

The train is rumbling to a stop. The name of the town on the station house is St. James. He hops down to the seat and then to the floor before taking to his heels and toes to get off the train in time. While three of the stores are self-explanatory, he's wondering about the one that isn't. Mapledorum approaches the front door and learns it's a restaurant. It's closed until dinner time. He reads the menu that's posted in the window. None of the dishes are listed. Mapledorum has never seen something like this before. He's intrigued because it's both an oddity and a curiosity. And when he realizes that's exactly what's motivating his interest, he sees that he's no different than anyone else. This is comforting and disturbing at the same time.

BILL OF FARE

UNIQUE FIVE-COURSE DINNERS SERVED NIGHTLY.

THE CUISINE IS DEPENDENT UPON THE AVAILABILITY OF THE DELECTABLE AND SEASONAL OPTIONS OFFERED BY MOTHER EARTH, CURATED PURELY AT THE WHIM OF THE CHEF. WHIMS AND WHIMPERS FROM THE PATRONS ARE NOT PERMITTED.

ROLL THE DICE. CHOOSE TO NOT CHOOSE.

WE HOPE YOU COME IN AND ENJOY THE UNEXPECTED.

$1.00

Mapledorum's eyes become as wide as the double zeros in the price. He'd never seen something so outrageously expensive. He believes he must've gotten off at the most frivolous town in the country. Then he wonders how divine the food must taste.

Mapledorum sees an alleyway between *Beauty* and *Rainbows* just wide enough for him to slip through. In the back, amongst the other cars in the parking lot, he sees a 1921 Ford Model-T that's been left to rust in peace. He climbs up the suspension and wiggles into a hole in the door that had rotted out.

Home sweet immobile home. He sprawls out on the seat and watches the full moon set over the black rainbow of the steering wheel horizon. Mapledorum thinks about the specificity of Ms. Mississippi's insistence that he go and find "Beauty in Rainbows." Not only did he physically go in *between* them, but it's how he found his new dwelling. His hunch is that his wish will be granted in the restaurant rather than the beauty shop, since the emphasis of the phrase seems to lie *in Rainbows* more than it may in *Beauty*.

Rainbows are objective to the eye, but subjective to the heart. Beauty is the other way around. In any case, he remembers that it will only happen if he doesn't believe in it. He wonders how this paradoxical notion will play out, but he's been writing a script in his head with block letters. Then his eyelids flutter like a fly in butter until his winged lashes become parenthetical dashes. Mapledorum rests very well.

CHRISTMAS DAY, AT NIGHT
1929

LONG ISLAND, NEW YORK

The next evening, Mapledorum is surprised to learn they are open on a day usually reserved for chimney mythology. He conspires to sneak into the restaurant. When all is quiet in the parking lot, he hides under a few leaves near the back door, waiting for the last member of the staff to leave. He presumes it will be the chef. So when he sees a toque poke outside, he gets ready to leap. The chef stands against the open door, which helps him remain vertical. He inhales the cool air. It's his first breath not infused with olive oil and oven flames. Then the chef exhales a sigh, wipes his brow of grease, and looks up to the sky. Mapledorum takes the chef's moment of serenity for his moment of opportunity. He's in. Not a champagne bottle pop later, the chef closes the door, and locks it with a jangling set of keys.

It's quiet and dark, save for the pilot flames, and the magic of bending moonbeams winding in through the windows. Mapledorum thinks it's a small restaurant for a menu with such grand ambitions. He counts eight seats at the L-shaped bar. The place is spotless, save for the Lincoln penny he finds next to the leg of a barstool. He picks it up, puts it behind his back, and tucks it into his pants. It gave him chills up and against his spine. Even though the law prohibits the sale of alcohol, the chef keeps a stash hidden from the nightstick brigade. The chef serves it to discerning guests in teacups with a wink and a finger across his lips.

In the kitchen, Mapledorum finds several apple pies set to cool overnight. He convinces himself that no one will notice if he takes a little corner of this circular dream. He turns his penny into a plate and starts to literally dig in. He scoops out a small piece of apple, a few handfuls of the filling, and a small section of the basket weaving. His sits down on the counter and takes his first bite. The dream becomes lucid.

His tongue swirls in cinnamon. He has a conversation with Johnny Appleseed. He tastes the deep amber notes of syrup and the blood of maple trees. Not surprisingly, maple is his favorite flavor. He savors hints of brown-sugared figs, confectionary peanut butter, caramel bourbon, cocoa-dusted dates, gingered marshmallows, and salted vanilla beans soaked in Sunday afternoons. He exhales and he rubs his chin as an ellipsis of spiced watermelon lingers for three hiccups.

Mapledorum licks his plate clean, becoming more intimate with Honest Abe than he would ever have expected. So enthralled he is by the experience, he looks for anything else he can try. Everything else is kept behind locked doors. He tries them all. About to give up, he bumps into a basket of the discarded linen napkins. After being used to wipe the corners of a mouth or veil an uneaten bite, each patron's napkin is tossed into the bucket by the busboy. The basket would be sent out to be laundered the next morning.

Mapledorum dives in and unfolds large canvases with brushstrokes flavored with mutton chops in apricot sauce, chicken breasts breaded with blueberries, sweet pepper soup stirred with an agave leaf, steak tartare capered with swinging jazz notes, and strawberry cheesecake topped with a Twizzler candle. He feels a bit iffy and icky about it, but no one is looking. So he has leftovers for dinner. He puts his tongue to the accidental artistry and enjoys a five-star, five-lick meal fit for Long Island royalty. He isn't necessarily full, but he's satiated.

He continues this routine every night. The chef leaves, Mapledorum jumps out from the leaves. He has plenty of water, a mosaic of napkins, and occasionally, some booze. He looks forward to the nights when the pies and pastries are left out to cool, but the best nights are when the chef drinks too much and forgets to put away an experimental dish. These are the nights when the elasticity of his clothes is tested. It makes tucking the copper plate into his pants a tighter squeeze. He also notices that the size of his heart has yet to subside since he visited Ms. Missy Mississippi.

After his midnight dinners, Mapledorum cleans the hard-to-reach areas in the kitchen. He figures it's the least he can do. One night, after scrubbing the top shelf of the spice rack, he feels entitled to drink some of the moonshine on the top shelf behind the bar. It's labeled XXX, each diagonal cross representing how many times it was distilled. This also entitles him to a hangover. When he hears the chef open the door with the melody of the morning, Mapledorum wakes up in a sleeping bag of paper napkins. The chef is singing *When You're Smiling*, the latest song by Louis Armstrong. Mapledorum isn't smiling; he's panicking. He makes his bed by taking it with him and hiding behind a recessed area by the bar sink. There he stays throughout the entire evening of service. He listens to the asynchronous parade of footsteps as the customers come and go. He listens to the servers describe the nuances of each course, speaking in tongues, and in the lingo of taste buds. Whatever it is, he's already fluent in the language.

Mapledorum is emboldened by the experience. And since he survives undetected, he decides it's time to make the move from the Ford Model-T to his secret place behind the bar. His new studio apartment has a bed of sponges, a bar rag comforter, and a steel wool couch. The living space is smaller than that of the sink, which also acts as a warm shower, a swimming pool, a hot tub, a dishwasher for his copper plate, and a laundry station.

Mapledorum's access to the art of food, whether in forgotten morsels, or impressionistically left on a linen napkin, is at an all time high. The clothes he stole from the stiff gentleman in the dollhouse are now too small. One night, he takes one of the fresh linen napkins and brings it to the kitchen. He takes the smallest of the chef's knives and becomes a tailor until daybreak. Mapledorum uses red and white butcher string to sew each piece together. In the end, he has a collared shirt, pants, a vest, and even a pair of slippers. The suit has the spirit of the American Pastime at the seams and a dapper bandleader's bop everywhere else.

He is now Mapledorum Trinket, the gentleman who always wears a white linen suit. This gives him sartorial confidence for the first time in his life. He further thinks that he'd blend in well if he ever got caught swimming in the basket of dirty linens at night. If anything, he might be too clean to belong there, and he'd surely be spotted. It's a chance he's willing to take in the name of fashion.

With his newfangled confidence, he gets more courageous when it comes to the pallet of palatable Picassos. Instead of waiting until the end of the night, he wants to lift the napkins right from the laps of customers while they're still relying on them.

He maps out a plan. The next night, he builds a small and nearly undetectable scaffolding under the overhang of the bar. He tests its fortitude by hanging and swinging on it like a set of monkey bars. His climbing muscles have kept their memory. He practices his technique of napery theft, swooping down like a gymnast on the uneven bars. Mapledorum sets up some napkins on the barstools and swooshes them away, similar to the way a daring server might pull away a tablecloth while keeping the dishes in place. He believes the best approach is to grab the center of the napkin, creating a temporary and miniature big top tent, before whisking it away like a long cape trailing behind him. The scaffolding also serves as a way to keep the linen from falling and potentially appearing as a little ghost under a sheet haunting the bar. But Mapledorum is not a puny poltergeist, nor is he a pocket-sized pickpocket. Mapledorum's act is simply to make something appear to disappear.

Instead of pretending to be the star of a radio show, now he is taking center stage in a magnificent theater. He's waiting in the wings while a man bellows over the crowd of a sold-out show. "Ladies and Gentleman, allow me to present our final display of talent for the evening! Please put your hands together for Mapledorum Trinket… The Lap Magician!"

So enthralled by his new venture, he decides to celebrate with a drink from the top shelf. He climbs up and tilts the XXX bottle into a thimble. As he positions the bottle back in place, he sees that there's also a label on the back, which is far more detailed than the front. What it says stings him more than the booze, like a beehive times a buzzillion. It's a handwritten eulogy from a soul six feet under and boxed in pine. The author is both unknown and curiously personal.

The tulips are mounting an uprising from my grave.
I'm looking up and watching their indigo roots right now.

My **photographic** future was in the palm of the beholder.
The mark of time was the **psychic** scar caused by the same hand
which rests upon my shoulder.

In my life, I eventually learned there was **beauty** in my needing.
It provided the light for my **readings**.

Memories no longer **mark** my tomorrow's lows.
Supposedly, I dream **in rainbows**.

But it's the tulips that will echo my short story,
their narrative whispered in the bloom of their ephemeral glory.

OMEGABET

"Love is the closest thing to laughter
and the closest thing to tears.
Love is the motive power of everything
in the universe that has beauty in it.
Love is the reason for everything
and the reward for everything."

HAROLD CLAYTON LLOYD, SR.

BOXXXING DAY
1931

ST. JAMES, NEW YORK

For two years and one day, Mapledorum performed nightly as the triumphant and secretive Lap Magician. He became so precise in his napkin lifting, he added the skills of a trapeze artist to his arsenal to keep his act challenging. Using a small bundle of toothpicks and fishing wire, the apparatus allowed him to swoop down to the floor if necessary. And it was necessary if a desired dish was on the ever-changing menu, and at the same time, under the barstool. While his ambition to be an oral surgeon had waned long ago, his tongue had earned a degree in culinary sensations. When he was presented to the stage (or more accurately, the catwalk), the voice that echoed in his head now proclaimed, "Ladies and Gentlemen... Put your palms together for... Wait! On second thought, keep your hands on your lap! Well, what matter will it be, for...

The One,
The Only,
The Undeniable and Unidentifiable,
The Understated and Over-satiated,
Swinging Savant... I present...

The Con Vivant!"

His audience was unaware they were witnessing a show. Mapledorum's two-year tenure wasn't without error. During a lull in the conversations, he almost lost his sublimity and title when he unknowingly licked an habanero pepper flake. His eyes watered most of the houseplants in town, his face turned as red a shy communist in a flower field of bleeding hearts, and his mouth wanted to ahh… ahh… achoo! But ever the stoic magician, Mapledorum held his decorum.

There were other areas of concern. He had to have an eye and an ear out for the guests who actually did use their dinner napkins as a sneeze snatcher. Mapledorum had found a few surprises that weren't on the menu and it destroyed his appetite for minutes on end. There were also numerous times when a guest would attempt a double dab, going back to tidy their mouth just moments after thinking they'd completed the job the first time. To swipe their napkin in between dabs would cause suspicion to rise. Mapledorum heard all of the restaurant gossip and knew more about the chef than he cared to, but he was surprised that the frequency with which diners asked for another napkin never pushed back the hairlines of the staff. He figured the servers and busboys were likely too busy to notice and the guests were too devoted to the meal to care.

Mapledorum was proactive, opting to be cautious by implementing a more precarious scheme. So adept he was, he began to incorporate the switcheroo, bringing back a fresh linen square to the guest before they knew it had been missing in the first place. True, he wanted to give back to the community of unaware benefactors, but he was also being selfish, as the linens were a renewable resource for the next spread.

Mapledorum perked up when the menu was on the messy side. On an evening he held quite dear to his little covetous heart, the first course included crumbly croissants twice buttered with sweet tomato jam. Mapledorum also salivated when customers came in talking dirty to one another. For example, if he heard a man apologize ahead of time to his date that he would be acting like a ravenous beast when the filet mignon with cuvée mignonette arrived, Mapledorum would become a steak stalker suspended from the scaffolding. Or if his date mentioned that she was feeling more stuffed than the turkey in front of her, he anticipated the possibility of an untouched bite hidden in the folds of her napkin. *Blown appétit!*

But… even with the success of his private circus act, something was eating at him. It wasn't merely flicking its tongue in his direction, it was taking bites out of him from the inside. Hearing terms like sweet pea, sweetie pie, honey pie, buttercup, sugar, pumpkin, peaches, and cupcake, didn't make Mapledorum the least bit interested in having another dessert. It made him sad.

He wished to be with someone too. Whether side-by-side at a bar counter, or face-to-face at a table, Mapledorum wanted to whisper those sweet somethings into a pretty woman's ear, and make her smile. And that would make him smile. And perhaps, all would be as right as rain in the world, even for a moment.

Now, a discerning reader of this story may be wondering that if this were truly the case, did Mapledorum wish for love when he was in the presence of Ms. Mississippi? Perhaps earlier, a reader of this story may have assumed that

Mapledorum wished to be taller—quite a bit taller. But that is not what he wished for. Mapledorum wished to be... smaller.

In the period when he was surrounded only by profound loneliness, he wished that he would become so small that he wouldn't exist at all. He at least wished to be small enough to climb into a bottle of moonshine and drown himself in liquid death. He wanted to stop trying to move forward on the unicycle of life, feeling as though he only knew how to climb up to the seat, or fall all the way to the underground. Mapledorum was, without a doubt, down and out. Now, after two circuits of the Earth, he feels inside out. His heart is not only worn on his sleeve, his aortic fluid is splashed all over his white linen suit.

Mapledorum tries to remember that a circular path is the longest way to get back to where you started. He thinks back to the time in his life when he took a path tangent to New York City. It was after he sat at the table opposite Ms. Mississippi. He would like to see her again, but Mapledorum realizes she is not here. Furthermore, with all of her glasses and gloves, her swirling robe, and the low lighting, he didn't really see *her*. And she didn't really see *him*. But Mapledorum believes they both *saw* each other, but that's as far as he wants to think about it.

What Mapledorum wants to think about, is his wish, or more specifically, the intention of the wish. So, he looks up to the bottle with three Xs on the top shelf. He knows he can't get inside of it, but he can put its contents inside of him. That would do the trick. He'll disappear into the clear. Isn't that how a magician should leave his audience? But he hasn't looked at that bottle since he read the cryptic words on the back. It was the only spirit that had ever haunted him.

Ridden with the sudden and desperate thrill of bowing out from the stage for the last time, Mapledorum begins the ascent to reach his demise. He thinks that even if the alcohol doesn't stop the pitter-pat in his ribcage, the landing surely will. But as he tilts the bottle, it rotates in such a way where Mapledorum finds himself holding each end of the back label, as if stretching his arms out to read a scroll. It feels like it's his own eulogy. He senses the tulips rising not above him, but within him. It's as if a smaller version of himself had been pine-boxed and buried in his heart. Whatever it is, it's telling him something he can't hear, but he can feel.

Mapledorum props the bottle back to its full height. At this exact moment, a motorcar pulls up and parks in front of the restaurant. It's quite an unusual time for any activity outside his own little world. The headlamps from the vehicle twinkle against the glass and refract into a million sparkles of light. He looks around and up at the kaleidoscope of hope surrounding him. It's the first instance, after all this time supposedly spent in rainbows, that he looked at the ceiling. Its color is a shade close to indigo, but it's not something he can name. Mapledorum has an epiphany. The moonshine is now his sunshine.

Standing on the top shelf, the performer inside Mapledorum has taken the stage once again. He looks down at his audience of none. He shakes his head. If this is his circus, he's the animal that put himself in his own cage. It's the only barred room that can be destroyed with memories. Knowing this, he reflects on the struggles of the colorful characters of the circus that helped raise him.

Mapledorum learned from them, was cared for by them, and loved them. In between performances, everyone dispersed into the town to attend to personal matters. Most of the time, it was for the simple pleasures of tasting the local cuisine, reading a book in the park, or going to a church to pray. Some of the time, it may have been to visit a doctor to ask about the rarity of their particular oddity. Cavity Patty, the woman born with upside down teeth, sought out the dentist in every town across the continent. Pineapple-Head Boy, his name unfortunately and plainly accurate, had optometrists looking the other way, while he looked every way. Pineapples have a lot of eyes, don't you know. Topsy-Curvy, the woman with breasts shaped like ampersands, kept her feelers out for reconstructive surgeons && curious semioticians. Jake the Ache, the young man with a third foot hanging between his legs, inquired with both the preeminent urologists and pediatrists of the day. For purposes of civility, and to match the one suit he owned, he was fitted for a single, yet very comfortable, Oxford shoe. The salesman remarked about the irony that his foot wasn't technically a foot long. Jake, an astute wordsmith, pointed out that every foot is indeed, by definition, a foot long. The salesman gave him the shoe for free. For what it's worth, he found the left one more amenable. Clutterfingers, a girl with a small hand on the end of each of her ten fingers, poked around town in search of philosophers. She wanted to know whether she had fifty fingers — or sixty.

Mapledorum remembered that Do-Re-Mi, the three-headed songstress, had issues with both hairdressers and priests. These are groups that don't typically share a Venn diagram. The issues with the hairdressers revolved around pricing. Were their listed service costs for one person — or for one head? The priests were presented with more of a theological dilemma. The conventional opinion was that she was born with a condition touched by the hot hand of Lucifer.

But the fact that she also was the physical embodiment of the cornerstone equation of Christian mathematics (3 = 1), caused the priests to scratch their collective heads into a blizzard of dandruff. Thus, in the cathedrals, she sang alone. Or, rather, she sang together. Or, maybe, she sang… never mind. See?

Medical practitioners, pious preachers, and professionals aside, when the circus members left their locomotive abodes and went out in public, they were treated with scorn. They were stared at with shielded eyes and covered gasps. No one wanted to see them living in harmony in the land of the supposedly free. But the hypocrisy emerged as soon as they appeared in costume or were stationed in dark tents to be viewed for enjoyment. For it was then acceptable to ogle, point, and laugh at the lineup of the freak show. Now they were performers, accidental comedians, a visual picnic for family entertainment. And not only were they deemed acceptable, the masses paid with their own earnings—possibly as a penance for their ignorant judgments—to make it so. To be truly accepted for who one is, the exchange of money is the antithesis of sincerity. In other words, there are no checking accounts opened in the denomination of $elf-worth.

Well, with that, the bars to Mapledorum's cage have been stretched out, and he feels free to leave. So free, he starts singing one of the new songs that he's heard playing on the radio when the chef is preparing his menu for the night. He belts out the chorus, "Dream a little dream of me…"

The other cage with an opening is made of Mapledorum's ribs. So he pulls his heart off his sleeve and puts it back in its home. He also takes off his suit, and wrings out the aortic fluid into a jigger behind the bar. He pours it back into his body for a shot of self-love. He's no longer down and out, nor is he inside out. Mapledorum is outside in.

So now, he grins, and takes an exaggerated and straight-legged step off the ledge. Then he turns his body around, grabs the ledge with his hands, and climbs back down to safety. Mapledorum sleeps soundlessly on his bed of sponges, soaking up his renewed sense of self. The show must go on for Mapledorum, The Lap Magician, The Con Vivant!

NEW YEAR'S DAY
1932

ST. JAMES, NEW YORK

Several days after his return to triumph, Mapledorum rises in the morning after his nightly vacation with the cousin of death. Now, when he looks up and sees the XXX on the top shelf, he smiles. On this morning, his grin is wider than usual, because today is his birthday. It's a new year for both Mapledorum and the entire planet. He thinks about taking off his linen suit and exchanging it for his birthday suit, but he decides to remain a gentleman.

During dinner service, Mapledorum is in full swing, swooping and swiping at will. But something causes his heart, and his trapeze, to freeze. There's a new pair of dangling legs that are next to an empty barstool. Upon the barstool beside the legs is a pile of glasses, gloves, and cotton balls. He counts seven pairs of each. He hummms to himmmself the initials of the mmmystic in his presence, followed by her name. "Mmm… It's Mmmiss… Mmmissy… Mmmississippi."

He can't see her face, which is nothing new, but he knows it is the she and only. Mapledorum imagines that she knows he is there. And it's in this moment that he starts to believe that his wish may come true. And he doesn't try to fight it. He had a twinkle of an idea just days ago. He'd hoped he could see her, but she was not there. Her words echoed in his cranium: "There is something *you* must do. You'll know what it is when it is not there." And like a cryptographer acting on instinct, Mapledorum knew what he must do. He had to kiss her.

It turns out that Ms. Mississippi was the first real woman he felt he could kiss. Perhaps it's because he was sitting across from her, or at times standing across from her, and he was fixated on her lips. They were also the only part of her skin that was bare. But fixated he was on the two lips. The *two lips*. Oh yes, the tulips were about to rise, indeed.

Mapledorum keeps his distance from her while she is having dinner. But while she's having the dessert course, he is deciding whether or not to take the riskiest of risks. He closes his eyes. Sure, he's thinking about the possibility of being exposed, but it's more about his nerves. He performs his own blind palm reading.

[Music Director: Please cue the chimes that sound like a fairy falling up the stairs.]

The answer from the master of puppetry returns with the following message: *The Future is Sweaty*. This is the first time he's felt the sensation. After all of the tall buildings he's scaled — ok, some of them only relatively tall — his nerves were always far from where their endings should anatomically be. But now, his palms are tropical rainstorms of perspiration. He worries about slipping off the scaffolding and landing on her lap, rather than lifting something from it. But our hero is a daring man.

Holding on for mere life, he swoops down to the south, and nips Ms. Mississippi of the cloth close to her loins. She does not react. Both surprised and relieved, he retreats to his hidden apartment to taste what she'd been tasting.

Mapledorum lays out the napkin. But instead of licking it, he looks at it. In fact, he is staring curiously and ironically at the oddity in front of him. The white linen, instead of providing a spectrum of both colors and tastes, is a monochromatic spread of reds. There are splashes of wine and words drawn with lipstick. Written in wax is the following message:

"Happy Birthday. I'll knock three times on the back door at midnight. Do let me in. We have much to discuss. I've been looking forward to sitting across from you again. - MMM."

Mapledorum vibrates his lips, "*Mmm…*"

Sure, this was a lot to ask of a small cylinder of lipstick, but it penned its marks without a smudge. Mapledorum gets a bit French with his kissing, tasting both her wine and her wax. *L'appétit vent en mangeant!* Perhaps this is his appetizer.

Mapledorum concludes his nightly act without a bow and waits for the arrows of time to point toward Corona Borealis, the northern crown constellation. He is feeling the magic of the events forthcoming. He undoubtedly believes his wish will be granted soon after the two hands join each other on the clock.

The first sound from the door occurs at 11:59:59 P.M. She's a little early.

Knock, [stroke of midnight], *knock, knock*.

JANUARY THE SECOND SECOND
1932

ST. JAMES, NEW YORK

Mapledorum watches Ms. Mississippi walk in and take a seat at the bar. He climbs up behind it and sits opposite her.

The mystic begins, "How are you, my dear?"

Mapledorum is just as mute as he was the first time they were in this position. It's not because his throat is dry, it's that he's never seen someone as beautiful with his own eyes.

She asks again, "Dear, how are you?"

Mapledorum answers, "I don't know."

She says, "Do you believe your wish will be granted and become true?"

"Yes. I knew it from the beginning."

"Did you wish to be taller?"

"No."

"Well, there's no time to waste, sugar. What did you wish for?"

"I wished to be smaller, honey pie."

"Then do what it is you believe you should do, cupcake."

"Alright, peaches. Pucker up."

"Are you sure you want to do this? Have you considered the consequences, buttercup?"

"Yes, pumpkin. Things are about to not change."

Ms. Mississippi thinks he misspoke, but grants him his retorts, calls them fine-line art, and purses her lips into a heart. Mapledorum leaps across the bar and stands with his chin tilted toward Saturn. She leans down toward Earth. They kiss a sweet kiss with hues of Zinfandel and dusted with zeppole zest. Zeppole zest is Italian for sugar. The result is a planetary impact and quite the astral display, despite their distance to the nearest star. After their lips part, Mapledorum stretches out to the size of a tree represented by the first two syllables of his name. This is to say, he grows to a height too tall for the restaurant. His head climbs, or rather tears, through the indigo-shaded ceiling. The constellations reveal themselves in a cosmic and slightly comedic display.

Mapledorum is at a loss for words. Ms. Mississippi is at a loss for an explanation. He sits down, now using the top of the bar as his seat. My, how the tables have turned.

Ms. Mississippi says, "I thought you would've wished to be taller, but I didn't expect anything like this!"

Mapledorum says, almost with satisfaction, despite feeling his internal organs still trying to catch up to their new home, "I didn't think this would happen either!" His voice is several octaves lower. "The truth is, I wished to be smaller."

Ms. Mississippi is starting to see what he is saying. "So you *believed* in what you wished for… on purpose?"

"Not at first, exactly. In the moment, I was at a place in my life where I wanted it to end. I wanted to become an electron. I wanted to become matter that didn't matter. I also didn't believe you at first, I'm sorry to say."

"While I'll try to veil my initial disappointment upon hearing that, I understand that taking a mystical woman wearing seven pairs of glasses seriously is quite the mental task."

"True. But when you told me to find beauty in rainbows, somehow I knew you were sincere. I adjusted my thinking. In that moment, I knew that your directive to not believe in the wish for it to come true, was real. I also know that I'm the type of person who wants to believe in the magical. So this was not a tall task at all." Mapledorum chuckles at his accidental wordplay. "Honestly, I didn't worry that I'd become smaller. I just thought that nothing would happen. Besides, it gave me a reason to kiss a beautiful woman for the first time."

"Oh, how romantically intuitive of you this is! But I have to ask you, have you ever wished to be taller?"

"No."

Ms. Mississippi is surprised yet again.

Mapledorum continues, "I *dreamed* of being taller. I *wished* to be smaller. There's a difference."

She ponders what he said. "I see."

"Well, of course you do. You're not wearing fourteen pieces of glass in front of your eyes."

Ms. Mississippi grins a mile-wide smile. "It's just an act, sweet pea."

"Everything in life is an act—an act of magic—if you give it any thought at all."

"That sounds quite cosmic of you to say, but I'm on the same page of the atlas."

"I figure that it stands to reason, that because we are within the galaxy of milk, ways, and means, everything that occurs here is a cosmic event, one bestowed by an unseen and anonymous charity."

The mystic adds, "The real miracle of life is that we don't recognize that everything that's ever happened in life *is* a miracle."

Mapledorum agrees, "Even from my new perspective, I know that we're all small wonders."

She lifts her chin up to him. "Yes, both significant wonders and insignificant wonders at the same time."

"It's not that our local solar system doesn't have the time to honor our daily triumphs, it's that it has too much time. It hasn't recognized we are here at all. What's important is that we recognize each other." And with that, Mapledorum leans down and kisses Ms. Missy Mississippi right on her lippilippi for the second time. It caramelizes all of the sugar on Long Island. After they part, he's a bit relieved that he didn't extend skyward any farther.

Ms. Mississippi's eyebrows lower in conjunction with her inquisitive tone. "Do you really want to remain this tall?"

Mapledorum laughs. It echoes in the restaurant and quakes the glassware. "Of course not."

She smiles back. "Good."

"What do you mean by that?"

"Because I have neck problems and… "

Mapledorum interjects, "…from wearing too many pairs of glasses?"

"Well, it's certainly not the gloves. But as I was saying, if you can keep your big mouth shut for a second, I have neck problems, and I'd like to kiss you again. And maybe a lot of agains after that."

Mapledorum is blushing, the roses on his cheeks blossoming to the size of two Valentine's Day bouquets. "I guess *dreams* do come true…"

Ms. Mississippi adds on, "…and maybe *wishes* too."

"Speaking of which, is there anything you can do about this? Meaning in the near future?"

Instead of providing an answer, she starts to recite a spell, her gestures invoking the spirits from beyond. Mapledorum's gaze is fixed on the contours and symmetry of her face. At the same time, he's wondering why it is that she has chosen him.

While writing in the air, this time with her finger ungloved, she says, "Zwix! Whavūts! Urk! Pŏn! Mahlick! Jig! Fed! Cabah!"

Mapledorum believes every nonsensical utterance. But is he supposed to? In his heart, which now has ten times the power of knowledge and capacity for love as it did before, the answer is yes.

Ms. Mississippi zips through the longest z-word he's ever heard. "Zwixwhavūtsurkpŏnmahlickjigfedcabah!" Then, in the reverse order as she did before, she points to the center of her ribcage, and then to her lips.

Mapledorum's finger, now the size of his former body, does the same. He realizes the spell began with how it ended the first time. Instead of the alphabet recited as one word, she recited it starting at the end. She recited the omegabet. The word appeared in a mist, formed a cloud, and rained itself down in drops and dots.

ZYXW VUTSRQP ONMLKJIHGF EDCBA

"Should I... do anything?"
She tells him, "Just wait."
"Is it going to be another two years?"

Ms. Mississippi giggles out of her temporary trance. "No. Maybe another two minutes. Reversing a curse takes less time."

"You cursed me?"

"No, I granted you a wish. Someone else cursed you before you were even born."

Mapledorum considers what she is saying, but he's more interested in the present. "But does that also reverse the love within the spell?"

"Yes. But don't worry, love is symmetrical and protected by the other letters, remember?" Ms. Mississippi shifts her rear end to the front end of the barstool. "I know something is on your mind. You're wondering why it is that I'm choosing you to lock lips with."

"Yes. I'm wondering, out of all of the people on this blue sphere, why do you desire *me*?"

She continues, "Ahh, what's more interesting than why I chose you, is why you chose that word. *Desire* is a word that should only be said in red. But to answer your question, it's because desire is irrational."

"And what of love? Is it also irrational?"

"Yes, but only when it's rationally thought out. Love can be all the colors and all the letters, forward and backward. But love, simply for the sake of love, is just someone's idea for what will fill the frame they've crafted in their mind."

He asks, "The frame?"

"Yes. The frame represents someone's expectations of what love should look like. But love is art. It's an erotic and faithful art charged with ionic question marks. It's an electric bolt that destroys your expectations. Show me a true artist who frames their art before it's finished, and I'll show you an unfulfilled lover."

Mapledorum asks her, "So, the full spectrum of love only can be sparked by the irrationality of desire?"

"Yes. Love is complex. At least the right kind is. The right kind is where desire is sustained. It's the only way the fire keeps burning. All fires will exhaust themselves without the infusion of sparks and oxygen. Even our sun will one day extinguish its own flames."

He asks her, "I assume the sparks are supplied by romantic thoughts and oxygen is supplied by wonderful conversations?"

"Yes. And yes and no. Conversations are fueled by curiosity, but they are spoken with carbon dioxide." Ms. Mississippi pokes at him, "Who was your science teacher?"

"I had two, actually. A sword swallower and a snake charmer."

"I should've guessed that. The oxygen is supplied by the oceans. Oceans of emotions."

Mapledorum processes all of this. "So, the fire in a relationship is dependent on the influence of water, just like the way opposing charges create the strongest attractions?"

"Yes. It's the most stable form of invisible connectivity. Desire is magnetic, ionic, and ironic." She pauses and smiles. "Did the sword swallower teach you about ions?"

Mapledorum winks, "She had a lot of trouble enunciating, so I'm not sure." Then he gets back on track. "So, to reiterate what's on my mind… why do you desire me?"

"Well, that's easy. It's simply because it doesn't make sense."

Mapledorum was hoping her answer would've included something about his handsome face and persistence in the presence of adversity. But he is content anyhow. He ultimately thinks it should be enough to know that someone loves you unconditionally. Because if the love is indeed unconditional, no one needs to know the reason why.

Both slowly and suddenly, Mapledorum shrinks to a height equal to Ms. Mississippi. The only thing that remains the same size is his heart. His white linen suit bumps visibly in accordance to the double thumps within. They embrace, their tongues kissing in planetary orbits, before they both look up to the night sky through the tear in the indigo ceiling.

Mapledorum says, "One thing the snake charmer taught me was that starlight is millions of years old, and that you'll never know how far your light will travel."

"That's the only science you'll ever need to learn."

And the two lovebirds looked up to the past and wondered what their futures held. They knew that it at least held each other.

They kept kissing until the sun came back around. According to the science taught by the snake charmer, Mapledorum understands that Earth is the center of the universe. And in this moment, there's not a person that would disagree with him, whether they are fearlessly irrational, or tame and prudent.

Perhaps it's instinctual, but Mapledorum wants to climb all over her. Ms. Mississippi wouldn't have been opposed to him roaming her mountainous regions, but everything was kept above the shoulders. It was all quite innocent. In the beginning, there is nothing more molten or passionate.

Mapledorum's focus lingered on Ms. Mississippi's tongue. It's where she wears her best lingerie. Since this is his first trip to the Mouth of France, he wants to savor the entire culinary experience. But with the finest and laciest linen on the menu now available to him, he has difficulty slowing down time. Mapledorum's only speed is lickety-spit. Upon finding dashes of her deserted dessert, he isn't sure which is sweeter, her lips or her last course. No matter the cause, his teeth hurt immensely. When Ms. Mississippi sees him wince too often for her to pretend not to notice, she asks him to open his mouth. She tells him to keep his tongue from misbehaving. She whistles cool gusts of air over each pearly rainbow of citrine-tinted ivory to see where the pain is originating. Mapledorum whines from molar to canine. Without magic as a medical option, he is acting like a small child.

Ms. Mississippi exclaims, "Oh honey-pie, we have to get you to an oral surgeon as soon as possible."

Definition

zyx·wvuts·rq·pon·mlk·jihg·fed·cba /ˈzwixˈwhaˈvūtsˈurkˈpŏnˈmahˈlickˈj igˈfedˈcaˈbah/

▸ **n.** The revelation and protector of desire, which is the only place where true love is found.

AFTERWORD, BEFOREWARD, DOWN, AND WAY, WAY, UP

"We are always the same age inside."

GERTRUDE STEIN

RO(+)YGB(+)IV

OCTOBER
2022

EAST SETAUKET, NEW YORK

On New Year's Day in 1982, a small wooden box was found hidden under the seat of a 1921 Ford Model-T after it was purchased at an auction in Amityville, New York. In the box were the following items:

One wine-stained linen napkin

Two miniature teacups with matching coasters

One miniature pitcher

Two ticket stubs dated September 22, 1925 to "P.T. Barnum's Greatest Show on Earth"

One dinner receipt marked "Paid" for $2.00

One Ten-Volume set of four-by-five-inch books, the contents of which have been carefully reproduced here, complete with any grammatical errors or inconsistencies contained in the original text.

Note: The tenth and final book of the set contains two first-name signatures on the last page: Mapledorum and Michelle. Missy is a common nickname for Michelle. Each has its own unique flair for the serif. The veracity and age of the signatures have been verified with carbon dating analysis, without objection from their peer group of scientists.

Also contained in the box, all of which were photographed and cataloged upon their discovery in 1982, are the oddities that have been the subject of much scorn from anthropologists and pragmatists alike. Most established professionals categorized them as being part of a well-performed hoax. However, some less-traditional scientists stepped out of the box—as it were—and claimed the contents therein were proof that time travel exists. Some members of the scientific establishment went so far as to call these dissenters, "Sci-Fientists." Other detractors claimed, in a rather clunky fashion, that they were practicing fake carbon dating.

Continuing with the contents of the box, there was a map to the whereabouts of the "Final Resting Places" of Mapledorum Trinket and Michelle Mississippi. A search for the locations proved difficult because they were deemed both nonlinear, and at times, nonsensical. The reason for this was later discovered by an astute cartographer. The plural use of the word "places" was not a typographical error, as many first believed. It turned out to be the geographical clue that led to the discovery that the couple had been laid to rest on a series of circus trains, continuously moving through time, and out of time. They are both still and in motion as you, dear reader, are learning of it.

There were two one-way tickets dated September 22, 2032 for travel on the P.T. Barnum Ferry, a vessel that crosses the Long Island Sound between Port Jefferson, New York and Bridgeport, Connecticut. The tickets each have a photographic image of both seaports. While the Port Jefferson location has looked more or less the same for decades, the Bridgeport image presents a seaside skyline that doesn't exist… yet. At the time of this printing, it has been verified in the city zoning records that development for a new harbor layout has been approved, and is in the design stage. The preliminary architectural renderings are eerily similar to that of the finished project pictured in the box of curiosities.

One of these tickets has the name Nicoletta, followed by a streak of color. The other has the name Tris, followed by a streak of a different color. The fact is that both colors are so unusual, they defy the laws of the known and visible spectrum. This is by far the most compelling finding inside the box, as there is no scientific explanation for them, whether by traditional or avant-garde methods.

Each color is "named" with one symbol, or character. The symbol following Nicoletta's name resembles a scribbled-in rectangle. After some typographic analysis, it turns out to be comprised of all of the letters of the alphabet superimposed upon one another. The symbol following Tris's name is the opposite, the edges of the rectangle only implied by speckled marks. This character is the absence of all of the letters superimposed upon one another.

Finally, there was a greeting card dated January 1, 1942. The inscription is as follows:

Dearest Mapledorum,
Happy Birthday to the man with the biggest heart we've ever seen or heard. Please send our best to Ms. Michelle, as well!
We've done our best in our travels, as you've requested, to let our imaginations grow beyond our limits and expectations. And for that, we thank you. We have found two, one hue for each one of you…supposedly.
With Darling Love,
Nicoletta & Tris

ALSO BY
LOUIS L. LASSER IV

UPRIGHT HARMONICA

Upright Harmonica is a collection of embarrassing short stories. It evolves with innocence, devolves with the loss of it, and revolves around a misconception about what a desk fan can do. It makes soap seem dirty. It looks up *Intimacy* in the dictionary under *B*. It's romanticism in spray paint and lyricism in shower steam scribbles. It will slow dance with your teenage memories. It will stand naked outside in the winter so it can cuddle you when you have a fever. In the middle of the book, there's a paper heart in search of a kiss-marked origami envelope.

It whispers to you in bed and tells you it's ok to fall in love. It admits that things won't be better tomorrow—it will take an imagined lifetime and generations of fantastic ghosts to follow. It has heart. It has ache. It wishes those two words would stay away from each other.

It gives you advice it doesn't take for itself. It goes to therapy for the couches. It's October and June in an August storm. It's a self-portrait with three shadows. It proves there are more than three tenses. It's a stick shift that drives the speed limit, but takes hard turns. It's a treasure hunt for a secret chapter hidden in the hollow of a tree. It also believes this description is too long.

It's the Alpha and the *Ohhhh*mega. It's risky and risqué, particular and peculiar, creative and meditative. It has a nostalgia for the future and a reverence for the now.

SHALIMAR

The Subterranean Travels to the Outer Space Dreams of Shalimar and Gable is a division sign with an identity crisis. It's a bowl of rock candy, a crystalline romance that wants you to bite, even though you know it's better when you lick. It's a love story in the amusement park of relationships that rides the truth like a rollercoaster spaceship. The admission is free, but the cost is sky-high. The ticket is golden, but also heavy. It loops and winds on a mosaic carousel where the horses run from their orbits and the music is better. It's a bubble bursting with adventure, told in conversations and reflective moments, leading to a discovery that two people belong on the same side of the mirror.

This novella takes fashion advice from trees, it doesn't return library books or compliments, and it leaps years and jumpstarts hearts. It paints your toenails with purple graffiti, spells sexy with two more xs, and it declares that romance is not dead, it's just taking a nap in the back seat of an old flying car. It can't hold still for pictures and it smokes cigarettes that rhyme. It records you when you snore and it pokes you in the mouth when you yawn. And it pronounces the first meal of the day like this: breafeks.

It's about the ironic collision of parallel lives. It's an accident that happened on purpose. And while it all happened just moments ago, it pretends to time travel. It's a beauty. And so is she.

DOUBLY BUBBLY

Doubly Bubbly is something that breaks all the rules. I mean, don't you want it to? Anyway, it's the kind of book that gets put in the corner, but also likes being there. It's a twisty straw to your mind, a swervy brainstorm of vapidity. It tells you to sit on its lap and ends up on yours. It's carbonated with apostrophes and ellipses. It wears something lacy when no one is looking. It's a meditative hallucinogen, a firecracker epiphany that converges to an infinite pillow. It overdoes it on the first date. It always guesses C. Some of its pages might be stuck together. But it's the truth. And you can finish it before you'd finish two martinis. Well, most of you.

WEDNESDAY NIGHT MEETING

Wednesday Night Meeting is a coming of age story disguised as a curvy math problem. Or maybe it's a second coming of age story. Or maybe it's a bucket list disguised as a gunshot mystery. Anyway, it makes you wonder why cleavage and the crucifix get along so well. It treats poetry like the vitamins in your mashed potatoes. It wanders through the concrete jungle with a reptilian boombox on its back. It hits all the flavor sensors on your tongue. It teaches you how to get into more bedrooms, that is to say, how to be more interesting. It's on the verge of making libraries sexy again. It makes a cup of coffee out of vowels and mixes cocktails with velvet. It starts with pheromone bones and the end is covered with graffiti and blood. And above all, it shows you how Earth is just one big magnet trying to pull us all together.

BUTTERSWEET MOTEL

Buttersweet Motel is a collection of short poems imprisoned in a red gum ball machine. Truly. These lyrical phrases are waiting for their sentence to end so they can predicate to the world just how sugary, spicy, and cinnamony it can be. Their cellmates are Atomic FireBalls, appropriately.

One quarter at a time, they'll bring heat to your tongue — or tingles to your mind. Arranged in the correct order, the poems tell a story where butter triumphs over bitter, and sleeps in on Sundays on a bed of pillow mints.

FORTHCOMING TITLES

DIVE BAR SUNRISE

Dive Bar Sunrise goes around and around, gets dizzy, and falls down. It orbits the Earth in squiggly circles. Sometimes it runs late and forgets to sing the dawn chorus. This is because it bartended last night and made too many pour choices. It's a cautionary tale of liquid friction, the whiskey sour that flows between living in death, and dying to live forever in one never-ending night. It's also a cocktail recipe book for those with an imagination. Please read irresponsibly.

SKY RIDE TAP

Sky Ride Tap is a love story about a clairvoyant sleepyhead named Tyrus. He's a tap dancer and he's in love with Cola. She sees the present clearly and is a gift to humanity. The story builds up to the opening night of the 2032 World's Fair in Chicago. It's also about the sustainability of chairs—and how that will affect the future of the universe.

ABOUT THE AUTHOR

Lou resides on a hill in East Setauket. He lives amongst chipmunks, blue jays, squirrels, and one woodpecker with whom he plays catch. The baseball is a peanut. He also lives with his grandmother, Marian. She is a marvel and a mezzo-soprano. He writes down words on paper; she lifts lyrics off the page. She also gives them rocket ship wings and lands them on a treble clef staff in the sky. Constellations sing for billions of years, don't you know.

Daydreaming at Midnight llc

Publishers

New York